P9-BIM-581

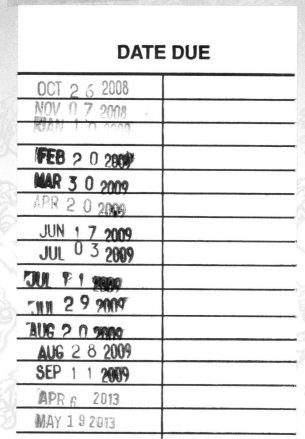

For my family, Chris, Cameron and Mallory:
You are my world and inspiration in every way.

For the little Grizzlies: May you always believe Montana is the best!

Thank you to Monte for being one-of-a-kind, and to
Miss Finley, whose birth started the wheels in motion.
~ JTN

The Great Monte Mystery

WRITTEN BY
Jennifer Newbold

ILLUSTRATED BY
Robert Rath

THE UNIVERSITY
OF MONTANA
PRESS

NEWBOLD
ENTERPRISES

Game time!

"Tomorrow is my big day,"
thought Monte.

2

"I can hear it now – the boom of the cannon, the beat of the music, the roar of my motorcycle, the yells of the crowd!"

Monte's fur tingled with excitement.

Tomorrow was the first Grizzly football game of the fall!

He could hardly wait to see the sea of maroon and silver and the excited faces of all the little Grizzly fans!

3

"**I** must get ready and pack my game bag. The players are depending on me," Monte said as he got ready.

"Let's see. What do I need to bring with me to the game?"

"Extra bandana – check!"

"Extra fish to eat – check!"

"Dancing shoes – check!"

"Football – uh oh!"

"Where's the football?"

Monte had always been the bear in charge of the game day football.

The players trusted him to keep watch over the ball until it was time to play.

Monte had taken extra special care of the football all summer, making sure it was properly inflated and stored safely in his cool, dark den.

"Oh where, oh where could that football be?" worried Monte.

"It's not in my den! It's a mystery!"

"I must retrace my steps," Monte reasoned.
"Certainly I can find it if I just search hard
enough. Now, where was I yesterday?
I'll start by looking there first,"
he planned.

Thinking back,
Monte recalled
that he had started
his morning by
picking berries on
the mountain.

"That's it! Maybe I left it
at the 'M!'" he exclaimed.

9

Monte began his trek up the mountain.

Huff, puff, huff, puff!

Monte marched up the switchbacks.

"Whew! Now where, oh where could that football be?"

Monte looked left and looked right, but there was no sign of it at the "M."

Monte Says

DID YOU KNOW?

The "M" is made entirely of concrete. The trail has 11 switchbacks and is 3/4 of a mile long.

"Oh, dear," said Monte, "I must
move quickly to find that ball
in time for tomorrow's game!"

"What did I do next? After
I finished picking berries
for breakfast at the 'M,'
I practiced my climbing
skills by scaling Main Hall."

"That's it! Maybe I left
it at the clock tower!"

Off Monte scurried, down the
mountain, straight to Main Hall.

Ding, dong, ding, dong!

The clock tower
bells rang loudly.

Monte pawed his way to the tip top of the tower.

"Whew! Now where, oh where could that football be?" Monte wondered aloud.

Monte Says

DID YOU KNOW?

Main Hall was built in 1898. The tower bells, which chime every ½ hour and hour, are called the carillon. There are 47 bells in the carillon.

He checked high; he checked low.
There was no sign of it at Main Hall.

Still retracing his steps from the
day before, Monte concentrated,
"Where did I go next?"

Monte Says

DID YOU KNOW?

The Clark Fork River is 327
miles long and has the largest
volume of any Montana river.
It carries an average 22,060
cubic feet of water per second.

"Aha! I remember! All that climbing of Main Hall made me very hungry, and I visited the river to catch some fish. That's it!"

"Maybe I left it at the Clark Fork River!"

Monte raced to the riverbank! *Swish, swoosh, swish, swoosh!*

The cold water was rushing quickly. "Whew! Now where, oh where could that football be?" asked a puzzled Monte.

Monte peered into the bushes and poked through the branches. There was no sign of it at the river.

Monte was becoming very concerned.

He was in charge of the football,
and he couldn't find it anywhere!

How would the Grizzlies play
their game tomorrow without it?
What would he tell the team?

And what about all the little
Grizzly fans? He didn't want
to let everyone down!

Monte took a seat on the riverbank
to think hard about where he could
have left the football.

Imagining yesterday's
events, Monte recalled,
"After I ate my trout
lunch at the river,
I went to play with my
little friends at Caras
Park. That's got to be it!"

"Maybe I left it at
A Carousel for Missoula!"

Monte hopped on his
motorcycle and cruised
to the Carousel.

The pipes sang playfully.
Ring, ting, ring, ting!

"Whew! Now where, oh where could that football be?"

Monte looked over the horses and under their hooves. There was no sign of it at the Carousel.

Time was running out!

Monte pictured the disappointed faces of the players and fans and wondered what he should do.

"Maybe I could tell them the ball popped while I was rehearsing my backflips," mused Monte.

"Or maybe they'd believe me if I said I gave it away to a deserving little Grizzly fan," he schemed.

"I know! I could tell them a Bobcat stole the ball!"

After a few minutes of thinking up all of the ways he could explain the missing football, Monte realized what he had to do.

He must tell the players what really happened.

Sadly, Monte shuffled toward the stadium.

26

The players were practicing hard for the next day's game, but as soon as they saw Monte, they rushed to greet him.

They were thrilled to see their beloved bear!

Monte reluctantly shared the bad news. "Fellow Grizzlies, I must report to you that somehow, somewhere, I lost the game day football you entrusted to me. I am very sorry and hope I can make it up to you."

"Hey, Monte," a voice called out.
"Is this what you're looking for?"

Sailing across the
football field came
the game day ball!

30

"I borrowed it yesterday for our practice. I must have forgotten to tell you," said Number 37 sheepishly.

Monte Says

DID YOU KNOW?

The Number 37 jersey is passed down from an older player to a younger player of his choice. The player that wears Number 37 must be from the state of Montana.

Monte did a backflip! Hooray!
The mystery was solved!

He hadn't lost the football after all.

He couldn't wait to cheer on his
Grizzlies at tomorrow's game!

The pounding of the drums, the shriek of the whistles, the thunder of the fans – he could hear it now . . .

Where did Monte go in Missoula?

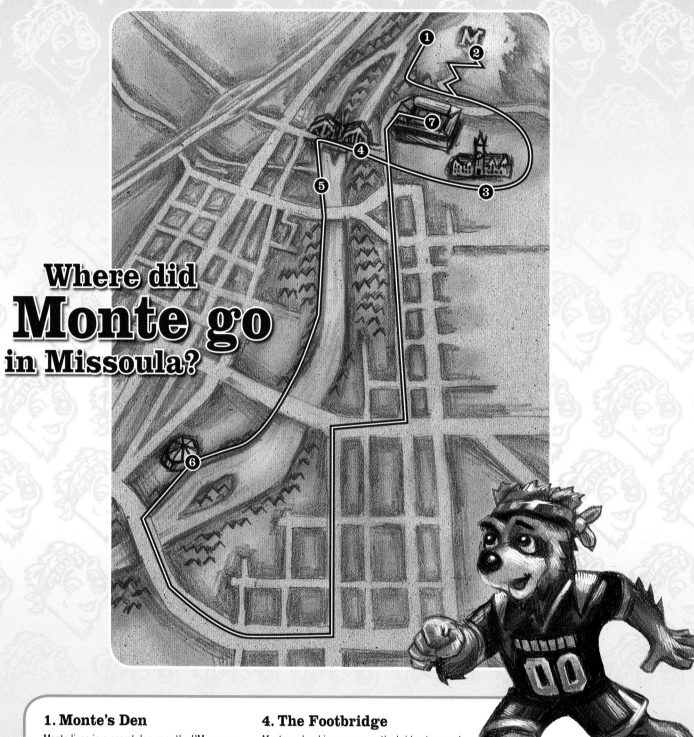

1. Monte's Den
Monte lives in a secret den near the UM campus.

2. The "M"
Monte treks up one of western Montana's favorite hiking trails.

3. Main Hall
Monte visits this historic building on the Oval in the center of campus.

4. The Footbridge
Monte makes his way across the bridge in search of some good fishing.

5. Clark Fork River
Monte searches for the lost football along the beautiful banks of the Clark Fork.

6. A Carousel for Missoula
Monte enjoys a magical ride at Missoula's renowned, hand-carved carousel.

7. Washington-Grizzly Stadium
Home of the Montana Grizzlies! Visiting teams beware!

Sing along to

The University of Montana

fight song!

Up with Montana, boys,
down with the foe,

Good ol' Grizzlies
out for a victory;

We'll shoot our backs
'round the foemen's line;

Hot time is coming now,
oh, brother mine.

Up with Montana, boys,
down with the foe,

Good old Grizzlies
triumph today;

And the squeal of the pig
will float on the air;

From the tummy of
the Grizzly Bear.

Jennifer
Newbold

Jennifer is a two-time UM graduate (BA '98, JD '03) and feels extremely lucky to call Missoula her home, so she and Monte can cheer on the Griz year-round! She also spends lots of time cheering on her family, which includes her husband, Chris (her partner in creating *The Great Monte Mystery*), and the next generation of Montana fans: son, Cameron, and daughter, Mallory. Go Griz!

Robert
Rath

Robert is an illustrator and designer living in Montana. He illustrated *First Dog: Unleashed in the Montana Capitol*, and has worked for clients such as Farcountry Press, Scholastic Books and Lucasfilm. His favorite project is keeping up with his family.

Many thanks and appreciation to those who helped bring *The Great Monte Mystery* to life (in alphabetical order): David Aronofsky, Kenny Dow, Jim Foley, Erin Egeland Fuller, Susie Galbraith, Liv Gregor, Rick and Susie Graetz, Tara Lind, Greg Malone, Ken Price and Carrie Schwartz.

ISBN 10: 0-9815760-2-8
ISBN 13: 978-0-9815760-2-2

© 2008 by The University of Montana Press and Newbold Enterprises, LLC
Text and illustrations © 2008 by Newbold Enterprises, LLC

Book design by Robert Rath.

Cataloging-in-Publication Data is on file at the Library of Congress.

Created, illustrated, produced and designed in the United States (Montana).
Printed in Korea.
Distributed by Farcountry Press.

First printing, July 2008